D0501773

Silly Steggy

Weekly Reader Children's Book Club
Presents

By Alison Cragin Herzig & Jane Lawrence Mali

Illustrated by Kimberly Bry

NEWFIELD
PUBLICATIONS
Middletown, Connecticut

This book is an original presentation of
Newfield Publications, Inc. Newfield Publications
offers book clubs for children preschool through
high school. For further information write:
Newfield Publications, Inc. 4343 Equity Drive,
Columbus, OH 43228

Newfield Publications is a trademark of
Newfield Publications, Inc. Weekly Reader
is a federally registered trademark of
Weekly Reader Corporation.
Copyright ©1993 Newfield Publications, Inc.

Text by Alison Cragin Herzig & Jane Lawrence Mali
Illustrations by Kimberly Bry
Editor: Stephen Fraser
Designer: Vickie McTigue Kelly
ISBN #: 0-8374-9801-5

Printed in the United States of America.

All rights reserved. No part of this book
may be reproduced or transmitted in any
form or by any means, electronic or
mechanical, including photo-copying,
recording, or by any information storage
and retrieval system, without written
permission in writing from the publisher.

T. J. McNeil had
four stuffed animals.
Every night they had jobs to do.

Monkey's job was to read
T.J. a bedtime story.

Pigger's job was
to get T.J. a glass of water.

Mister Bear's job
was to turn out
T.J.'s light.

All T.J.'s animals had
night jobs.
Except for one.
Steggy had no job.

One night, after Monkey closed
the book and Pigger brought the
glass of water, T.J. called a meeting.
"Last night I saw a monster
in my room," he said.

"I don't like monsters," T.J. said.
"Someone has to chase it away."
Monkey and Pigger and Mister Bear
and Steggy stared at him over
the edge of the covers.

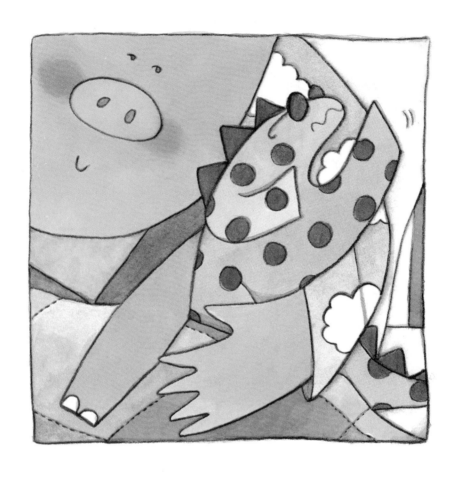

Finally Steggy raised a paw.
"I can do it," he said.
"Okay, Steggy," T.J. said. "You do it.
The monster is tall and bumpy."

Mr. Bear turned out the light.
Then Steggy saw the monster.
It was tall all over and bumpy
on top. Steggy jumped.

"No, Steggy," T.J. said.
"That's not the monster.
That's my lamp.
The monster flaps and bangs."

Monkey and Pigger and Mister Bear
pulled the covers up to their chins.
"I can do it," Steggy said.
He backed slowly off the bed.

Then he heard it.
It was flapping and banging.
Steggy crossed his toes
and pounced.

"No, silly!" said T.J.
"That's not the monster.
That's my window shade.
The monster smells stinky."

Monkey and Pigger
and Mister Bear pulled
the covers up over their noses.
"I can do it," Steggy said.

He inched his way
down the edge
of the comforter.
He snuffled under the bureau.

He nosed under the chair.
Then he smelled it.
It was a stinky monster smell.
Steggy held his nose and dove.

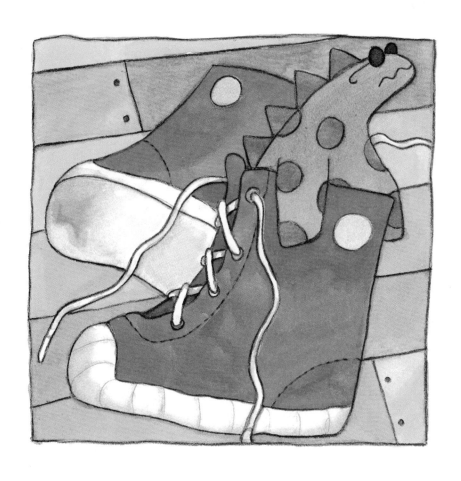

"Silly Steggy!" said T.J.
"That's not the monster.
Those are my sneakers.
The monster is really, really scary."

Monkey and Pigger and
Mister Bear pulled the covers
up over their heads.

"I can
do it,"
Steggy said.
But he wished
it wasn't so dark.
He wished monster
chasing wasn't so
hard. Most of all he
wished he was snuggled
in bed with everyone else.

But he was determined
to chase away that

tall, bumpy, flappy, bangy, stinky,
really scary night monster.

"I can do it," Steggy said.
He shinnied down the bed post.
He looked high and low.
He listened right and left.

He smelled inside and out.
Then he crossed his toes and
held his nose and put up a paw
and charged.

CRASH!

"Hooray! You chased that
monster away," shouted T.J.
Monkey and Pigger and Mister Bear
came out from under the covers.
"From now on", T.J. said,
"monster chasing is Steggy's job."
He picked Steggy up and gave him
a hug. Monkey and Pigger and
Mister Bear moved over
to make room.

Steggy snuggled under the covers
next to T.J. McNeil. He smiled from
ear to ear. "I have a job," he said.
"And I can do it." Then he closed
his eyes and went right to sleep.

CREEEEEEAK!